W9-ASZ-905

On the First Day of

Summer Vacation

On the First Day of Summer Vacation • Copyright © 2019 by HarperCollins Publishers • All rights reserved. Manufactured in China. • No part of this book may be used or reproduced in any manner whatsoever without written permission except in the case of brief quotations embodied in critical articles and reviews. For information address HarperCollins Children's Books, a division of HarperCollins Publishers, 195 Broadway, New York, NY 10007. • www.harpercollinschildrens.com • Library of Congress Control Number: 2018937924 • ISBN 978-0-06-266852-3 • The artist used Photoshop and watercolor paint to create the digital illustrations for this book. • Typography by Chelsea C. Donaldson and Honee Jang
19 20 21 22 23   SCP   10 9 8 7 6 5 4 3 2 1 ❖ First Edition

To my granddaughter Grace, who LOVES summer vacation!
Love, T.R.

For my wonderful mum
—S.J.

On the First Day of Summer Vacation

by Tish Rabe

pictures by Sarah Jennings

HARPER

An Imprint of HarperCollinsPublishers

On the first day of vacation

I had so much fun

playing all day in the sun!

On the second day of vacation

I had so much fun

riding my bike

and playing all day in the sun!

On the third day of vacation

I had so much fun

going for a hike,

riding my bike,

and playing all day in the sun!

On the fourth day of vacation
I had so much fun,

LEMONADE

25¢ a glass

selling lemonade,

going for a hike,

riding my bike,

and playing all day in the sun!

On the fifth day of vacation

I had so much fun

SLEEPING OUTSIDE!

selling lemonade,

going for a hike,

riding my bike,

and playing all day in the sun!

On the sixth day of vacation

I had so much fun

building castles in the sand,

SLEEPING OUTSIDE!

selling lemonade,

going for a hike,

riding my bike,

and playing all day in the sun!

On the seventh day of vacation

I had so much fun

learning how to swim,

building castles in the sand,

SLEEPING OUTSIDE!

selling lemonade,

going for a hike,

riding my bike,

and playing all day in the sun!

On the eighth day of vacation

I had so much fun

helping my team win,

learning how to swim,

building castles in the sand,

SLEEPING OUTSIDE!

selling lemonade,

going for a hike,

riding my bike,

and playing all day in the sun!

On the ninth day of vacation

I had so much fun

paddling a canoe,

helping my team win,

learning how to swim,

building castles in the sand,

SLEEPING OUTSIDE!

selling lemonade,

going for a hike,

riding my bike,

and playing all day in the sun!

On the tenth day of vacation

I had so much fun

going to the zoo,

paddling a canoe,

helping my team win,

learning how to swim,

building castles in the sand,

SLEEPING OUTSIDE!

selling lemonade,

going for a hike,

riding my bike,

and playing all day in the sun!

On the eleventh day of vacation

I had so much fun

catching fireflies,

going to the zoo,

paddling a canoe,

helping my team win,

learning how to swim,

building castles in the sand,

SLEEPING OUTSIDE!

selling lemonade,
going for a hike,
riding my bike,
and playing all day in the sun!

On the twelfth day of vacation

I had so much fun

seeing whales go by,

catching fireflies,

going to the zoo,

paddling a canoe,

helping my team win,

learning how to swim,

building castles in the sand,

SLEEPING OUTSIDE!

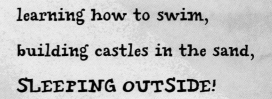

selling lemonade,

going for a hike,

riding my bike,

**and playing all day
in the sun!**